In Search of a Quiet Place

Dr Gargi Sinha

Acknowledgement

I must start by thanking Dr

Priyanka Sahni Verma MBBS

(LHMC, New Delhi),

MS (Obstetrics & Gynaecology)

Dip RANZCOG,

Fellow of the Royal Australian

College of General Practitioners

(FRACGP)

For allowing me to borrow her

arduous fellowship exam journey

for writing the book -In Search Of a Quiet Place. When she passed her FRACGP exams, we went for an evening cup of coffee, and she showed me some corners and benches in Perth, Western Australia, temporarily serving her as a study table. At that moment, I realised a mother's challenge for higher studies is unique in many ways. On the one hand, to pass the exam, a candidate needs time, but on the other hand, a mother also needs a quiet place. So, I decided to explore more from Priyanka and her extraordinary journey. Her perseverance and dedication towards her profession are exemplary. I am incredibly grateful to her for giving me creative freedom and letting me design the book's main character, Pari and her journey.

Contents

Chapter One

Shifting focus

"Mom! Look at the Spider-man mask," giggled two-and-a-half-year-old Abir who quickly ran up beside his mother, Pari, and climbed onto her lap to look through her books.

"Oh, Spider-man! Wow!" Pari

instantly switched her focus

from her own books to Abir.

She knew that she should be

focussing on revising for the

fast-approaching fellowship.

But instead, she put her books aside and cuddled Abir and started playing with him.

Meanwhile, Pari's kind-hearted nine-year-old daughter, Samira, entered the room and gently held little Abir's hand. "Abir, come. Let's play with the balloon," she said, pulling her brother off their mother.

Samira turned towards Pari and gently whispered, "Don't worry, Mom, concentrate on your work. Papa and I will take care of Abir."

Pari kissed her daughter's forehead and said, "Samira, always be the sweet girl that you are. I am so proud to be your mother." Samira smiled and nodded at her mother,

then led Abir away.

After marriage and

motherhood, everything

changes. Being responsible

for young children is a huge

task which is beautiful,

exhausting, and frequently

unpredictable. Often,

caregivers have to drop

everything when their

children are in need.

But, for a parent, there is no

column on the examination

form that allows you to select

"parenthood" as an excuse for

not coming prepared for the

test.

The harsh reality of the

current examination system is

that no matter what phase of

life you're in, or what

struggles you're currently

facing, the timeframe and

conditions for turning in a

professional paper remain the

same for every candidate.

Deep inside, a mother

(especially a mother of young

children) knows that she is

significantly disadvantaged

compared to other candidates

when taking an exam.

Frustration and hopelessness

are common phenomena for

individuals who bear

demanding roles at the same

time as sitting such vital

examinations. But perhaps

parenting provides a unique

resilience and resourcefulness.

Instead of counting problems, a mother usually looks for a solutions.

Chapter Two

Taking a break

It was late and Pari held Abir

in her arms, gently swaying

and humming a sweet tune,

but her thoughts constantly

shifted back to her exam and

career. She wanted to commit

to the long and arduous

process of the Royal College

exam, but she felt agitated and

hopeless. Like an elastic band

being stretched further and

further in opposite directions,

Pari was scared the pressure

would make her snap.

Meanwhile, little Abir was

asleep on her left shoulder.

She gently carried her son up

the stairs and laid him down

in his cot. She looked down at him, studying his face and wishing she could slow down time; he was growing so quickly. She was startled out of her musing when her phone started vibrating in her pocket. *Who is calling in the middle of the night?* Pari thought. When she saw the name of the caller, a huge smile crept onto her face. She picked up the phone and, trying to control her excitement, she whispered, "Hello! Wait a minute, I've just put Abir down, let me go to another room".

A few moments later, Pari spoke again, "Rupa! I'm so glad to hear from you. How are you? "Rupa was Pari's best friend and a batchmate

from their MBBS days, and

she was currently practising in

America.

Rupa's voice was a welcome

distraction from Pari's inner

conflict and soon she felt

completely relaxed. Although

the geographical distance

between them was huge, they

stayed as close as ever and

were giggling at each other on

the phone like schoolgirls.

Rupa told Pari that she had

planned a get-together in the

UK with some of their old

classmates and wanted Pari to

join them. Pari hesitated for a

moment and thought about

Samira and Abir. She was

used to turning down these

kinds of things because of her

duties as a mother. *The kids need me more*, she would say to herself. But this time, Pari promised Rupa she would join them and then hung up the phone.

After all these years of studying, exams, work, and raising a family, Pari was looking forward to a much-needed break; something that was just for her, so she could

free herself of responsibilities

for a little while and

rejuvenate. There would be

plenty of big projects

throughout her career, and this

was the perfect time to take a

break before getting stuck in.

So, Pari decided to leave Abir

and Samira with their father in

Perth and planned a solo trip

to the UK to meet Rupa and

their friends. When it came

time to go, it was hard for Pari

to leave the country alone, but

she knew if she didn't take

some time for herself, she

would suffer from burnout

and not be able to give her

best effort to her career or

motherhood. She saw the trip

as an opportunity to "fill her

cup."

Pari's husband Vicky was

incredibly supportive of her

decision, and he was happy to

stay home and look after Abir

and Samira, rather than take

them both on a long-haul

flight overseas. He knew how

important it was for Pari to let

off some steam and enjoy

herself after years of hard

work.

However, not everyone

supported Pari's decision or

perhaps could even

understand the necessity of

going overseas just to meet

with friends. But Pari

followed her heart, and her

husband and daughter fully

supported and encouraged

Pari's adventure.

Soon, Pari met with her

college friends away from

work and family

responsibilities. For Pari, this

was the best decision and one

of the best experiences of her

life. The trip also strengthened

the foundations of her

marriage by setting an

example of what genuine

support meant for each other.

Often in a marriage, we tend to believe that choosing a vacation means running away from marriage and responsibilities. The opposite is true - taking time to recharge and avoid burnout is what makes you a better spouse and parent. For a woman, taking a break from her daily routine helps to

improve her emotional and

mental well-being.

Chapter Three

The journey to the royal road

The royal road to achieving

the Fellowship of the Royal

Australian College of General

Practitioners (FRACGP) was

full of hurdles and obstacles

for Pari. Dreaming of the

prestigious post-nominal letters of FRACGP by her name, initially, seemed an impossible task due to the stringent paperwork requirements by the college for overseas doctors.

However, after looking through the college website, she understood that once the training was complete and she passed the exams, she would be eligible for FRACGP. But Pari wanted to know more details about the training and examinations. So, she asked several people she knew if they had any leads on where to gather more information.

Finally, she found a female doctor who was happy to answer her questions about the FRACGP examination and apprised her that she needed to sit three different tests to be successful.

"Three separate tests?" Pari asked, "And it's compulsory to pass all three to obtain the FRACGP?"

The female doctor nodded to confirm.

Pari felt like she was standing at the bottom of a huge, steep mountain with big boulders hurtling down towards her as she struggled to the top. She paused and thought about not pursuing the extensive curriculum of Australian General Practice. She already had the Australian AHPRA registration after clearing

daunting examinations of
Australian Medical Council
examination that consist of
Multiple choice questions and
clinical assessment.

But a voice inside her head
that was louder than the voice
of doubt told her that it was
just another challenge - and
she liked challenges. She
made up her mind to push

herself towards the arduous

journey of the royal road of

FRACGP.

Chapter Four

In search of a quiet place

Pari's previous degrees

obtained in India, narrated

voluminous past of her hard

working and perseverance.

Facing exams wasn't nothing

new to her, appearing for

various examinations was

what she had done to achieve

32

status of a medical

practitioner. For Pari,

preparing exam means putting

mind and soul into

preparation to obtain result.

But Pari sensed her

determination remained same

but her surrounding shuffled

considerably.

She still holds stamina of

continuously studying for

hours with her full focus. But

where is the time with

children and full-time work.

Despite her challenges in

balancing role of motherhood

,profession and studies, for

Pari there's no better feeling

than holding baby for the first

time. Pari always reinstated

the feeling of pure joy when

she remembered her wedding

and the birth of her two

beautiful children.

 Pari was aware being a

mother sounds easy, but it

was anything but easy.

Imagine waking up in the

middle of the night with a

crying baby who needs a

diaper change and a toddler

tugging at your hand. Or

being cautious the entire day

because the young ones don't

understand that a switchboard

isn't a toy.

Undoubtedly, exam

preparations required a set

routine and time but for a

mother of toddler like Pari

one additional challenge

added for preparation? Where

to search for a quiet place to

prepare for exam ?

Managing time was one part,

and the other was finding a

quiet place to study.

In the entire day, she could

manage 3-4 hours where she

had no disturbances. But the

search for a quiet place soon

turned into an expedition. At

first, she started in her

bedroom. But the incessant

crying of the baby meant that

she could barely concentrate.

She had help from her

husband, who would take care

of the kids for a few hours

during the day.

A blessing in disguise came

when her neighbors offered

their help with the children.

Sania and her husband Ravi were great with the kids. Part and Sania had been great friends ever since they had moved into the neighborhood. Sania suggested that Pari take her children to their homes so she could have some quiet time for studying. However, despite that, something else would come up in line with household duties that she had

to take care of. It was only

after some time that she

realized that a change in

environment would help her

settle into studying better.

A five minutes' drive from

her house was a coffee shop.

And it was the only place

where she could find some

peace and quiet. The coffee shop had a great atmosphere, with live music playing in the background and no noise pollution whatsoever. Pari would sit there with her books and notes, occasionally getting up to get herself a cup of coffee. Initially, it felt great to sit and start studying without any disturbances.

Pari, however, soon realized that the coffee shop was not the best place to study. Even though it had a great atmosphere, there were too many people around, making it difficult for Pari to concentrate and focus on her studies.

Nature is the best resource, right? That's what she thought next. A park nearby, with a dense tree cover and plenty of open space - perfect for her to set up her makeshift study corner. She would often take her children with her so that Sania and Ravi could take a break from looking after them. What started as a good idea, soon turned into a full-fledged study session in the park. Pari would quickly set up her study space - a picnic rug, some books and notes, and a cup of coffee - and spend hours studying undisturbed.

The only problem with this was that not all parks were open at all times. Towards the evening time, the parks would get dark, and she had to wrap up her session and head back home. Her search for a quiet place then led her to the fast-food joint near her house - McDonald's. Commercial places like these are open 24 hours, making them an ideal spot for studying late into the night. The ambiance of the place was quite pleasant, with soft music playing in the background and plenty of tables around for Pari to set up her study corner. However, this was quite a challenge for her. She had to take care of her children and juggle between looking after the kids and studying for her exams. A few times, she even heard murmurs about how strange it was for someone with a family to be sitting at McDonald's late into the night studying.

The last month preceding the exam was a bit of a struggle for Pari initially, until she figured out quite a few places where she could study without any distractions. She would often juggle between her home, the coffee shop, the park, and McDonald's - studying little by little at each place, until finally completing her studies right before her exams.

The motivation and determination that Pari had were exceptional. With her kids in tow and a great friend like Sania, she managed to make time for studying even amidst the chaos of daily life. She realized that there is no substitute for hard work and dedication. However, even with all of this, a quiet place is a must for anyone who wants to find success. And Pari eventually found hers in

the form of four different

places - her home, the coffee

shop, the park, and

McDonald's.

Chapter Five

The final letter arrived

On the exam result release

day, Pari was anxiously aware

that one little word deciding

her fate. She can't stop

thinking which word going to

display: pass or fail? Her heart

was pounding, and her hands

were shaking while logging

her RACGP account. The
nerves were rattling through
her as she was clicking
through screens to check her
candidate number. She
calmed her nerves and
prepared for the worst by
muttering to herself, "There
will always be a next time."
She closed her eyes as the
screen loaded with the results

and recalled her mum's face and her blessings. Pari felt at ease and gradually opened her eyes to see the result delivered by the Australian College of General Practitioners. She rubbed her eyes twice and checked the screen multiple times to make sure she could see the word 'PASSED' written in front of her name. It

wasn't a mistake. She'd done
it. Tears rolled down her
cheeks as she felt an
overwhelming sense of
excitement and relief. In her
joy, she thanked God for the
blessing.

Finally, Pari received her
letter that stated that she had
successfully completed all the
requirements for the award of

Fellowship of the Royal Australian College of General Practitioners and her name was entered on the Register of Fellows.

Later, one fine Sunday in October, she was invited to join the RACGP Fellowship Ceremony that formally recognised the hard work and dedication put forward by doctors to achieve the

prestigious FRACGP.

> *To some, a degree
> obtained while
> pursuing higher
> education is
> merely a piece of
> paper that silently
> hangs on the wall
> inside a wooden
> frame. But when
> keenly observed,
> the proudly
> hanging testamur
> represents a
> journey of courage
> and perseverance
> despite all odds.*

In search of a quiet place

Pari found her inner

strengthen to accomplish her

dream to obtain the

Fellowship of the Royal

Australian College of

General Practitioners.

Printed in Great Britain
by Amazon

24980010R00039